Fly, Ladybug, Fly!

written by
Katie Zimbaluk
MS, OTR/L, M.Ed.

illustrated by
Carmen Corrales

This edition first published in 2024
by Lawley Publishing,
a division of Lawley Enterprises LLC

Text Copyright © 2024 Katie Zimbaluk
Illustration Copyright © 2024 Carmen Corrales
All Rights Reserved

Hardcover ISBN 978-1-960137-59-3
Paperback ISBN 978-1-960137-61-6
Library of Congress Control Number: 2023952335

Lawley Publishing
70 S. Val Vista Dr. #A3 #188
Gilbert, AZ 85296

LawleyPublishing.com

For my Grandma Mae, who shared her love of ladybugs with me, and to my daughter, who inspired me to write this book and will always be my little love bug. —KZ

Where monkeys swing in groves of trees
and parrots soar across the sky,
there lives a tiny ladybug
who has a single wing to fly.

The ladybug is climbing high
and spots a hungry bumblebee
who's gulping nectar
down for strength,
then Ladybug begins to plea.

"Oh, Bee, I'd love your sound advice. Can you tell me how to fly?"

"You need to nourish like I do, to gain your strength for soaring high."

The bug considers Bee's advice
and quickly looks for plants to eat.
She makes a large and tasty meal,
then eats and feasts until complete.

As Ladybug attempts to flap
her tiny wing with all her might,
she gives it everything she's got
to take this most important flight.

FLIP!

FLAP!

FLOP!

The ladybug is falling fast
and loops in circles down the sky!
"My single wing is not enough!
Without a wing, I'll never fly!"

The bug is crying many tears
and sadly thinks about her grief,
until she spots a dragonfly
who's calmly resting near a leaf.

"Oh, Dragonfly, I need advice
to fly and get me off the ground."
"Ascend the ants' enormous hill
Then jump up high and off their mound."

The bug decides to climb the hill
and finds the very tippy top.
Although she's feeling rather scared
she shuts her eyes and takes a hop.

As Ladybug attempts to flap
her tiny wing with all her might,
she gives it everything she's got
to take this most important flight.

FLIP!

FLAP!

FLOP!

The ladybug is falling fast
and loops in circles down the sky!
"My single wing is not enough!
Without a wing, I'll never fly!"

The bug is dusting off her wing
when many colors catch her eye.
She spots a lovely butterfly
who's soaring low across the sky.

"Oh, Butterfly, I'm feeling stuck,
I really need to learn to fly."
"My friend, you need a gentle breeze
to lift you high across the sky."

She thinks of Butterfly's advice
and feels a cool and gentle breeze.
She hunches down and waits to fly,
and soon enough, she lifts with ease.

As Ladybug attempts to flap
her tiny wing with all her might,
she gives it everything she's got
to take this most important flight.

She hits a bulky stack of leaves
when out of nowhere, comes a thought!
Her mind begins to wander fast
about the many lessons taught.

The bug begins with Bee's advice
and eats a meal before her flight.

She's feeling nourished,
good, and strong,
then grabs a leaf
and holds on tight.

She thinks of Dragonfly's advice.
With leaf in hand, she climbs the hill.
She lays the leaf beside the peak,
then climbs on top and holds it still.

She clings on tight and hunches down
and thinks about the butterfly.
Then comes a cool and gentle breeze
that lifts her high across the sky!

WEE!

WEEE!

WEEEE!

The bug and leaf are soaring high!
The critters shout,

"Hooray!

Hooray!"

The bug exclaims to all her friends,

"I'm flying—
in a
different
way!"

Katie Zimbaluk worked as a teacher and occupational therapist before becoming an author of children's books. Specializing in working with children of all ages and various diagnoses, she has a passion for helping children reach their goals and embrace their differences.

Katie spent time volunteering for the government-funded program AmeriCorps National Civilian Community Corps, which drove her career in the direction of helping others. After completing her Master of Elementary Education degree, Katie taught second, third, and fourth grades. She subsequently completed her Master of Occupational Therapy degree and worked as a pediatric occupational therapist assisting children in both clinical and school settings.

When not writing, Katie enjoys creating art and has won several awards for her artwork, including becoming the first-place scholarship recipient for her artwork that was used on all advertising for the Arizona Scottsdale Culinary Arts Festival. You can connect with Katie on Instagram at the_ot_author or visit her website, www.katiezimbaluk.com for additional information.

Carmen Corrales is an illustrator and children's book author. Her books have been published in Spain, Mexico, Colombia and South Korea. After graduating from art school she decided to specialize in children's illustration. Carmen loves to create stories with her drawings about animals and nature. She lives in Baja California, Mexico with her sister and their furry family of 21 rescued animals including dogs, cats and a pig.

Want more insightful, empowering, fun children's books?
Want activities and links to go along with the story?
Visit us at lawleypublishing.com

For updates and info on New Releases follow us at

 lawleypublishing   @kidsbookswithheart  LAWLEY PUBLISHING

Printed in the USA
CPSIA information can be obtained
at www.ICGtesting.com
CBHW040805271024
16327CB00057B/20